D0183940

For Martin and Wren – C.A.

For Toms everywhere – G.A.

EGMONT
We bring stories to life

First published in Great Britain 2018 by Egmont UK Limited
The Yellow Building, 1 Nicholas Road, London W11 4AN

www.egmont.co.uk

Text copyright © Corrinne Averiss 2018
Illustrations copyright © Gabriel Alborozo 2018

The moral rights of the author and illustrator have been asserted.

ISBN 978 1 4052 7820 1

A CIP catalogue record for this title is available from the British Library.

THE BOY ON THE BENCH

CORRINNE AVERISS
ILLUSTRATED BY GABRIEL ALBOROZO

EGMONT

The boy on the bench was Tom.
The bench was in the playground.
And the playground . . . was full.

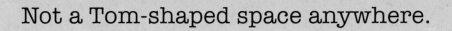

Not a Tom-shaped space anywhere.

"It will be time for dinner soon,"
said Tom's dad. "Don't you want to go
on the climbing frame?"

"In a minute . . ." said Tom.

Tom shuffled
closer to his dad.
There were children
EVERYWHERE.

Every inch of the slide.

Every single monkey bar.

Every swish of the swing.

Not a Tom-shaped space ANYWHERE . . .

. . . no matter how you looked at it.

Tom watched the roundabout spin a circle of arms and legs.

"Do you want a go?" asked Dad.

"In a minute . . ." said Tom.

Swings squeaked, a dog barked,
a giggle followed a squeal.

A boy shouted, "Nee-nor, nee-nor!" as he thundered
around the playground being a fireman.

The sounds poured into Tom's
ears and jangled in his head.
"Hello . . ." he whispered,
to see if anyone heard.

They didn't.
No Tom-shaped
space in all this noise.

But the bench was still.
And Dad was quiet.

Tom watched as the fireman hosed down the slide.

"Swooooooooooosh!"

Everyone screamed as they were soaked in water!

It was funny. Tom laughed
and shuffled to the edge
of the bench . . .

. . . and then he shuffled
right back again. Back to Dad.

"Who wants to play
fire rescue?"
shouted the fireman.

A girl with a teddy did.

So the fireman flung
her teddy to the top of
the climbing frame!

"Help!" said the girl.
"Someone save my teddy!"

But the fireman had already
found another fire to put out.

Tom could climb, though.
Perhaps he could rescue her teddy . . . ?

Tom was off the bench!

He climbed
the ladder.
One bit
at a time.

Tom didn't hear the fireman, the cheering girl or the barking dog.
Just the rubbery squeak of his own shoes as he climbed . . .

. . . to the top!
He tucked the teddy tightly under his arm
and step by step returned him to safety.

"Thank you!" said the girl.
"Will you play on the roundabout with me?"

Tom nodded, and together they hopped on.
Hands gripped, feet pushed, a *wooooo* followed a *weeeee*!

And when their last spin was spun,
Tom raced his friend to the monkey bars . . .

Now they were jungle monkeys swinging from tree to tree, with an *ooh ooh ooh* and an *eeh eeh eeh*!

"Time to go home!" called Tom's dad.

"In a minute!" said Tom,
and he smiled.

Because somewhere
in all the noise, between
the swish of a swing
and the squawk of
a squeal . . .

Tom had found
a Tom-shaped space!